# PATCH PUFFIN

## and the HATCHLINGS

BY BRIGID O'CONNOR　ILLUSTRATED BY CARLY FOWLER

ISBN: 1500418579
ISBN 13: 9781500418571
Library of Congress Control Number: 2014912170
CreateSpace Independent Publishing Platform
North Charleston, South Carolina

## DEDICATIONS

· · · · · · · · · · · · · · · · · · · · · · · · · · · · · · · · · · · · · · · · · · · · · · · · · · · · · · · · · · · · · · · · · · · · · · · · · · · · · · · · · · · · · · · ·

For Kathy Kinne, best friend, best example of a great momma for all her "hatchlings", you have always encouraged people to reach for their dreams, this one's for you! - BC

For my Mom and Dad, this hatchling couldn't have done it without you! - CF

*Brigid O'Connor*

## ACKNOWLEDGMENTS

My thanks to my parents, William and Mary Lou O'Connor, my sister Kathleen Benzaquin without their help this book would never have happened. To my friends in Pleasure Island's organizations of Island Women and the Sea Turtle Project, especially Jean S. and Susan P., Wanda F., and Jan V. who have welcomed me with open arms and hearts into their lives. I am blessed every day to live by the ocean with its natural beauty and wonderful people. BC

One day, as Patch the Puffin was flying along the beach, he came upon an old friend.

Busy at work pushing sand behind her was Tomisina, a large green sea turtle. "Hello Mrs. Turtle, it's been a long time since I've seen you," said Patch.

"Why, Patch how big you've grown, you are becoming a fine puffin indeed," exclaimed Tomisina Turtle. Patch fluffed his feathers with pride as he sat down to watch. "Mrs. Turtle, what are you doing with that big pile of sand?" asked Patch.

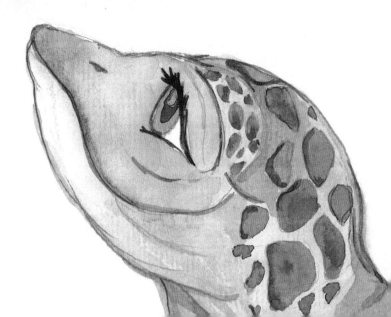

"Well Patch, I come back to the beach each year to lay a new clutch of turtle eggs" said Tomisina Turtle as she piled sand over the deep hole. "I will cover them up to keep them warm and safe, soon they will be ready to hatch, and make their way to the sea." Tomisina Turtle gave a final pat to the sand pile and turned to leave.

"Wait!" shouted Patch "aren't you going to stay to watch them hatch?" "Oh no Patch, I must return to the sea, and hope that my little ones will make their way safely to the water. This is what sea turtles have been doing for thousands of years.

Don't be sad Patch, sometimes I get to see my hatchlings when I return to the island to lay more eggs, that is a special day indeed!"

"Good bye Patch, be a good puffin" said Tomisina Turtle as she slipped into the sea, raising her flipper in a friendly wave, she dove deep into the water.

Patch settled down next to the sand pile and wondered about the little hatchlings. Overhead some hungry looking sea gulls were also watching it. "Mrs. Turtle worked so hard to make a warm, safe nest for her eggs, but if she can't watch them who will keep them safe?" thought Patch.

"I must keep these eggs safe, it's up to me now" and with that Patch gave the loudest puffin squawk he could make frightening the hungry sea gulls away.

Patch's friends, Terry the Tern and Rolo the Seal Pup, found him sitting on the beach. "Gee Patch, you look so serious, what's the matter?" asked Rolo. "I've got a big job to do and I could use some help" said Patch. He explained to his friends all about the sand pile.

"Patch, we can help you, the three of us can scare any sea gulls away!" said Terry as she excitedly flew around them. "That's great!" exclaimed Patch and the three friends settled in and watched the sand pile, and waited,

and waited...

and waited!

"Gosh, Patch." grumbled Rolo, "how long does it take? It feels like we've been watching this sand pile forever!" "I don't know Rolo, Mrs. Turtle never told me how long they take to hatch. But I hope it's soon." said Patch as he glanced again over the turtles nest.

Wait! Was that a tiny flipper poking through the sand? Suddenly, the face of a tiny sea turtle appeared and quickly began to make its way down the beach to the water's edge.

"Look there's more!" squeaked Terry. The sand pile moved and shifted when the baby sea turtles began making their way out of the nest.

"Hurray!" said Patch, "they've arrived! Let's help them find their way to the sea before any of those hungry sea gulls come back."

Rolo swam into the water to guide them towards the safety of the deeper currents. Soon, the very last hatchling made it into the water.

Just like its Momma, it gave a friendly wave before disappearing beneath the water. "Whew!" said Patch, "that was hard work, I hope they find their way."

"Look Patch! Look Terry!" said Rolo as he bobbed in the water. There far off shore was Tomisina Turtle, making her way back to the sea after another visit to the island. She gave the three friends a wave and called out "Thank you Patch, I'm so happy to see my hatchlings swimming around me, you truly are a noble puffin!"

Patch felt so proud that he and his friends had helped the turtle hatchlings safely make their very first journey to the sea.

Authors Disclaimer: According to scientific data, sea turtles do not return to their nests or wait to see their hatchlings. For the purposes of my story I have created an ending although unlikely, would be wonderful to think might happen!

For more information on Puffins, visit:
ProjectPuffin.org

For more information on Sea Turtles, visit:
seaturtleproject.org
seaturtlehospital.org
Pleasureislandseaturtleproject.org

When visiting coastal beaches, please remember to:

Fill in any holes before you leave the beach area.

Dispose of all trash in designated areas.

If you see a nesting turtle or hatchlings appearing, call the local sea turtle project or 911.

If you own or rent a home facing the sea, please turn off outside lights at night as they confuse the turtles and hatchlings from returning to the sea.

Many beaches along our coastline have "Turtle Talks" during the summer months. These are fun, educational presentations for the whole family to enjoy. Contact your local sea turtle project for dates and locations.

Made in the USA
Charleston, SC
05 September 2014